Julian Scott

The Song of the Ancient People

Julian Scott

The Song of the Ancient People

ISBN/EAN: 9783744767279

Printed in Europe, USA, Canada, Australia, Japan

Cover: Foto ©Andreas Hilbeck / pixelio.de

More available books at **www.hansebooks.com**

Julian Scott
1892

The Song of the Ancient People

By Edna Dean Proctor
with Preface and Notes by John Fiske
and Commentary by F H Cushing
Illustrated with eleven Aquatints
By Julian Scott

Boston and New York
Houghton, Mifflin and Company
The Riverside Press, Cambridge
M DCCC XCIII

The Riverside Press, Cambridge, Mass., U. S. A.
Electrotyped and Priuted by H. O. Houghton & Co.

List of Aquatints

Preface

IT is customary to speak of America as
the New World ; and to the white race of
men it is indeed a world that has but re-
cently been made known, and in which
European civilization has begun to flourish
under new conditions. The scene of the
political and social development of New
York, of Manitoba, or of Chili, is very
properly called a New World. But there
is another point of view from which America must be regarded as preëminently an
Old World. The people of aboriginal
America, when visited by Europeans in
the time of Columbus and Cortes, were in
a stage of social development somewhat
such as the people of Europe had passed
through and left behind some centuries
before the city of Rome was built, or the

Greeks had begun to reckon time by Olympiads. The parallelism is not in all respects complete, but it is very striking and instructive.

There can be no doubt, I should think, that the gradual differentiation of the races of mankind took place after man had become distinctively human, and in all probability this differentiation began in the Eastern hemisphere. In other words, the aborigines of America probably migrated to this continent either from Asia or from Europe. But these things happened a great while ago, probably long before the Glacial Period, and — as I believe it will ultimately be proved — even as far back as the Pliocene age. The ancestors of the Red Men doubtless made their way hither on foot during some one of the many periods when North America was joined both to Siberia and to northern Europe. Their race-peculiarities may have been developed partly in the slow dispersal and migration, still more in the countless ages during which they have dwelt upon American soil. For a length of time, in comparison with which the interval between the building of Solomon's temple and that of the World's Fair edifices at Chicago seems extremely brief, the isolation of America from the Eastern hemisphere was complete. All attempts at tracing an Asiatic or European influence upon the thoughts, the customs, the arts of pre-Columbian America have failed utterly. There is little room for doubt that the state of society found on this continent by the Spaniards was in all its phases and in every particular a purely American growth. Wherever it presented points of resemblance, either deep-seated or superficial, to social phenomena in Europe or Asia, the true explanation is to be found in the limited range of culture and the similarity in the workings of the human mind at different times and places.

That similarity is often very remarkable, as the comparative study of languages, of folk-lore, and of institutions abundantly teaches us.

Society in America, then, and society in the Eastern hemisphere followed each its own course in utter independence and ignorance of the other. There were many parallelisms, both curious and instructive, between the two; as, for example, the general organization of society in clans, phratries, and tribes, and even such special correspondences as the function of the phratry in prosecuting criminals, among Aztecs and Iroquois, as among the ancient Greeks and our own Germanic forefathers. The divergences are quite as interesting as the parallelisms. Social development in America proceeded much more slowly than in Europe; and the advance toward civilization among the Mexicans, Mayas, and Peruvians had begun to take on a very different aspect from anything ever seen in the Eastern hemisphere. The causes of the slowness of social progress in ancient America were complex, but one very important cause may here be singled out for mention. The dog, used chiefly for hunting, was from time immemorial domesticated in both hemispheres; but of those agricultural animals — the ass, horse, camel, ox, goat, sheep, and hog — the New World had not one. The effects of this difference were very profound and very far-reaching. The longest strides towards civilization that ever were taken in the Old World were the evolution of the patriarchal family in place of the old maternally-related clan, and of private wealth in place of the primitive communism, and both these strides were closely connected with the keeping of flocks and herds. In the Mediterranean countries these strides had been taken before the times of Agamemnon or of Abraham. In aboriginal

America, where there was never a pastoral stage of social development, they were never taken at all. Of the vast mass of ideas and sentiments originating in indissoluble wedlock, with the accumulation and inheritance of private property, the minds of the Red Men were destitute. In this respect, and in general, society in the Western hemisphere lagged at least sixty or seventy centuries, and perhaps more, behind society in the Eastern. The dim past that lies back of European history is to some extent brought before us in the Red Man contemporary with us. Except for changes wrought by contact with white men, his mental furnishing and his social arrangements are in many ways like those of our own forefathers in that far-off time when the Aryan mother-speech was forming. Such, at least, is the legitimate inference from all the facts before us; and thus it appears that in a very deep sense America may be regarded as preëminently an Old World, and its native inhabitants as especially an Ancient People. If not in all senses more ancient than ourselves, they are unquestionably more old-fashioned.

Among the aboriginal Americans there were, and still are, great and important differences in degree of culture. The highest grade reached anywhere was a barbarism without iron or the alphabet, but in some respects simulating civilization, and unquestionably different from anything ever seen at any time in the Eastern hemisphere. Without beasts of draught, the Red Man had no use for a plough or a wheel-carriage. Agriculture, properly so called, was impossible, but a certain kind of rude horticulture was practiced, in which the ground was scratched and hoed, and maize, pumpkins, tobacco, and other vegetables were grown. Chief among these plants was the maize, the Indian corn, most beautiful and beneficent of the cereals, and as typical of ancient American culture as the cow was typical of private property (*peculium*) among the early Aryans. No other plant is so intimately associated with the whole aboriginal history of the Western hemisphere as Indian corn. Far more than any other plant it is the emblem of America. In the southwestern portion of the territory of the United States, and thence southward along the Cordilleras as far as Lake Titicaca, the aborigines cultivated this cereal systematically and on an extensive scale with the aid of irrigation. This improved horticulture was the chief basis of the semi-civilizations of the Cordilleras. With the increase of population clans grew to large dimensions, and learned to build for themselves great communal fortresses of adobe-brick and ultimately of stone. These pueblo-castles and their neighboring gardens of maize are typical of the most advanced society in aboriginal America, as

tents and herds of cattle were once typical of the most progressive societies in'
the Eastern hemisphere. The city of
Mexico, which was so bewildering to its
Spanish visitors and conquerors, was doubtless a collection of such communal fortresses.

The Pueblo Indians of New Mexico and
Arizona are still surviving examples of
this advanced aboriginal society. In many
respects they do not seem to have attained
to as high a stage of semi-civilization as
the Mayas and Mexicans, but they are to
be classed with these peoples as belonging
to a stage far more advanced than the partly
hunting and partly horticultural Indians
of North America, such as the Creeks or
the Iroquois. Of the Pueblo Indians the
principal surviving groups are those of
the Rio Grande valley, the Zuñis of New
Mexico, and the Moquis (or Hopi) of Arizona. The two last-named groups have
been less affected by contact with white

men than those of the Rio Grande. In many respects the Zuñis are the most characteristic and interesting of all. But the pueblos least modified by contact with white men are surely those of the Moquis, with whom my friend Mr. Julian Scott lived for a year or so, and from whom he has taken the subjects of some of his most charming sketches in the present volume. Few Americans realize how highly our country is favored in having within its limits such communities as those of the Moquis and Zuñis. Our land is certainly lacking in such features of human interest as the ruins of mediæval castles and Grecian temples. But we may be to some extent consoled when we reflect that within our broad domains we have surviving remnants of a state of society so old-fashioned as to make that of the Book of Genesis seem modern by comparison. In some respects the Moquis and Zuñis may be called half-civilized ; but their turn of thought is still very primitive. They are peaceful and self-respecting people, and in true refinement of behavior are far superior to ourselves. We have still much to learn from them concerning ancient society, and we ought not to be in too great a hurry to civilize them, especially if they do not demand it of us.

Miss Proctor's noble and spirited poem speaks for itself and tells its own story. As a rendering of Moqui-Zuñi thought it is a contribution of great and permanent value to American literature. So it was regarded — as I think it permissible to tell — by our beloved poet Whittier, who has just left us. Miss Proctor had entitled her poem simply "The Ancient People," but when Mr. Whittier listened with keen pleasure to the reading of it, he said at once that it should be called "The Song of the Ancient People;" for do we not hear their own voice and feel their own heart's beat in every line? The poet's instinct was here as sure as if he had been an ethnologist.

The poem, I say, tells its own story; but as Mr. Cushing also feels a lively interest in that story, we could not lose the opportunity to have him further elucidate and enrich it in his "Commentary of a Zuñi Familiar." Somewhat as the old hymns of the Veda had their commentary, half poetical, half philosophical, in the Upanishads, so in a somewhat similar way — though all such comparisons need qualification — does "The Song of the Ancient People" find further interpretation at the hands of the adopted priest of the Zuñis.

For such phrases and allusions in the poem as seem to need explanation for the general reader, I have appended explanatory notes; and in these notes, so far as the pictures are concerned, I have embodied sundry materials furnished by Mr. Julian Scott. While my own share in the

Preface

book has been a brief and humble one, I
shall never forget the delightful sense of
comradeship aroused in working with such
friends and allies. But I am sure we
should all feel this little book to be sadly
incomplete and ungrateful, if in its Preface
no mention were to be made of our beloved and revered friend, Mrs. Mary Hemenway, to whose enlightened and untiring
zeal American archæology, no less than
the later history of our country, is more
deeply indebted than is ever likely to be
generally known.

JOHN FISKE

The Song of
The Ancient People

The Song of
The Ancient People

WE are the Ancient People;
  Our father is the Sun;
Our mother, the Earth, where the
    mountains tower
  And the rivers seaward run;
The stars are the children of the
    sky,
  The red men, of the plain;
And ages over us both had rolled
  Before you crossed the main; —
For we are the Ancient People,
  Born with the wind and rain.

And ours is the ancient wisdom,
  The lore of Earth and cloud: —

The Ancient People

We know what the awful lightnings
    mean,
Wí-lo-lo-a-ne with arrows keen,
   And the thunder crashing loud; —
And why with his glorious, burning
    shield
   His face the Sun-God hides,
As, glad from the east, while night
    recedes,
Over the Path of Day he speeds
   To his home in the ocean tides;
For the Deathless One at eve must
    die,
To flame anew in the nether sky, —
Must die, to mount when the Morning
    Star,
   First of his warrior-host afar,
   Bold at the dawning rides!
And we carry our new-born children
    forth
His earliest beams to face,

And pray he will make them strong
    and brave
As he looks from his shining place, —
Wise in council and firm in war,
And fleet as the wind in the chase; —
And why the Moon, the Mother of
    Souls,
  On summer nights serene,
Fair from the azure vault of heaven
  To Earth will fondly lean,
While her sister laughs from the tran-
    quil lake,
  Soft-robed in rippling sheen;
For the Moon is the bride of the glow-
    ing Sun,
  But the Goddess of Love is she
Who beckons and smiles from the
    placid depths
Of the lake and the shell-strown
    sea; —
Why the Rainbow, Á-mi-to-lan-ne,

From the Medicine lilies drew
Orange and rose and violet
Before the fall of the dew, —
The dews that guard the Corn-maids,
And the fields keep fair to view;
But the Rainbow is false and cruel,
For it ends the gentle showers,
And the opening leaves and the ten-
der buds
Like the ruthless worm devours,
And still its stolen tints are won
From the blanching, withering flow-
ers;
The Morning Star, the Sun, and the
Moon —
Yá-o-na, Ya-to-k'-ya, and Mó-ya-
tchûn —
Bring bounty and love and life,
But the Bow of the Skies and the
Lightning
With famine and death are rife,

4

And we paint their forms on our ar-
    row-shafts
And our shields, when battle lowers:—
We know what the breeze to the pine-
    tree sings,
And the brook to the meadow fair,
And the eagle screams to the plunging
    streams
Where the cliffs are cold and bare,—
The eagle, bird of the Whirlwind-God,
    Lone-wheeling through the air;
And we can charm the serpent's tooth,
    And wile the wolf from his den,
For the beasts have told us their se-
    crets
    Close-kept from other men,—
The mighty beasts that rove the hills,
    Or lurk in cave and fen:
The bear in his gloomy cañon;
    High 'mid the crags, the sheep;
The antelope, whose endless files

O'er the far mesa's rocky isles
  Their silent marches keep;
The lordly bison with his herds;
  Coyote swift and sly;
The badger in his earthy house
  Where warm the sunbeams lie;
The savage mountain lion
  With his deadly roar and leap: —
And, when the serpent has sought his
      lair
  And the thunder peal is still,
We know why the down of the North-
      land drifts
  O'er wood and waste and hill;
And how the light-winged butterflies
  To the brown fields summer bear,
And the balmy breath of the Corn-
      maids floats
  In June's enchanted air;
And when to pluck the Medicine flow-
      ers

On the brow of the mountain peak,
The lilies of Té-na-tsa-li,
That brighten the faded cheek,
And heal the wounds of the warrior
And the hunter worn and weak;
And where in the hills the crystal
stones
And the turquoise blue to seek;
And how to plant the earliest maize,
Sprinkling the sacred meal,
And setting our prayer-plumes in the
midst
As full to the east we kneel, —
The plumes whose life shall waft our
wish
To the heights the skies conceal;
Nay, when the stalks are parched on
the plain
And the deepest springs are dry,
And the Water-God, the jeweled toad,
Is lost to every eye,

The Ancient People

With song and dance and voice of flutes
  That soothe the Regions Seven,
We can call the blessed summer
    showers
  Down from the listening heaven !
For ours is the lore of a dateless past,
  And we have power thereby, —
Power which our vanished fathers
    sought
  Through toil and watch and pain,
Till the spirits of wood and wave and
    air
  To grant us help were fain ;
For we are the Ancient People,
  Born with the wind and rain.

And, year by year, when the mellow
    moons
  Beam over the mountain wall,
Or the hearths are bright with the
    piñon fires

And the wild winds rise and fall,
Our precious things to their shrines
    are brought
That the tribes may be brave and
    strong ;
And round our altars with mystic rite,
Vigil and fast and song's delight,
    And measured dance we throng, —
The dance and prayers of the A′-kâ-kâ
    That peace and joy prolong.
Of the Wood-Gods' flesh these altars
    To the Great Six Realms we
    frame : —
For the North, of the Pine, whose yel-
    low heart
    Nor blasts nor snows can tame ;
For the West, of the Willow, whose
    leaves are blue
    As they toss in the breeze at morn ;
For the South, of the Cedar, ruddy-
    hued,

9

From whose bark the flame is born ;
For the East, of the Poplar, downy-
    white
In the dawn of the gladsome year ;
For the Realm Above, of the Juniper,
    That climbs to the summits clear ;
And of Laurel Root, for the Realm
    Below,
    Deep-hid in the cañons drear ; —
Frame that the Beings Beloved may
    come
    And their forms and thoughts re-
    veal ;
For naught, from the heart through
    vigils pure,
    Will the Mighty Ones conceal.
Our richest robes and brightest hues
    For the watching sky we wear,
With necklace-beads and eagle-plumes
    Above our flowing hair,
And yellow pollen over us blown,

And of the two immortal youths,
　Twin children of the Sun,
Who eastward led their faltering bands
To find where morn begun, —
　To gain the stable, midmost lands,
And the trembling borders shun;
And of Pó-shai-an-k'ya, the master,
　Whose help we never lose,
Who bade us turn from hate and guile
　And ever the noblest choose,
And said that whoso smites a man
　His own heart doth bruise.
Of Earth and the Gods he taught us, —
　How slope and plain to till,
And the streams that fall from the
　　mountain snows
　To turn and store at will;
And how to trace the glorious Sun
　North and south to his goal;
And straight, when the body's life is
　　done,

Set free the prisoned soul!
His voice was sweet as the summer
    wind,
  But his robe was poor and old,
And, scorned of men, he journeyed
    far
  To the city the mists enfold, —
Far to the land where his treasured
    lore
  And secret rites were told;
And there with a chosen few he dwelt
  And made their darkness day,
Till lo! while his words yet thrilled
    their hearts,
Unseen, as the summer wind departs,
  He vanished in mist away! —
Passed to the splendor of the Sun,
He, the divine, the gracious one,
  To hear our prayers for aye!
And still our holy fires we keep,
  And the sacred meal we strow,

With many a prayer to the Gods of
    the air
And the Gods that dwell below, —
The Gods of the Great Six Regions:
    The yellow, dreadful North;
The West, with the blue of sea and
    sky;
The ruddy South, where the corals lie
    And the fragrant winds go forth;
The pure white East, whose virgin
    dawns
    Lead up the conquering Sun,
While stars grow pale and shadows
    fail,
    For the shrouding night is done;
The Over-world, where all the hues
    In radiant beauty shine;
The Under-world, more black and
    drear
    Than the gloom of the deepest
    mine;

Julian Scott
1892

And the Middle Realm, where the
    Mother reigns
  And binds them all in one ; —
Prayers in the words our fathers
    knew,
And prayers that voiceless steal
To the Holder of the Trails of Life
  And thought to thought reveal !
For the clamorous cry unheard will
    die,
While, swift as light, ascends on high
  The silent heart's appeal.
And we offer the pledge of sacrifice
  To lull the earthquake's wrath,
And hush the roar of the whirlwind
  Abroad on his furious path, —
Turquoise blue, and ocean-shells,
And the soothing, spicy scent that
    dwells
  In the rare tobacco leaves,
And macaw-plumes to guard from ill

And bring us store of sheaves;
Nay, in the time when thunders
    pealed
And Earth swung to and fro,
Our dearest maids to the angry Gods
    With fervent heart would go,
That the perfect gift of a stainless life
    Might still the vengeful throe ; —   ·
For our fathers were wise and pure of
    breath,
The breath that is soul the word be-
    neath,
    And all their ways we know.
And when at last the shadow falls
    And the sleep no thunders wake,
By the dead a vase of water clear
    For the parted soul we break,
Giving the life again to the Sun
    Through Kâ-thlu-el'-lon's Lake;
And, facing the east, the body lay
    In our mother Earth to rest,

Where dews may fall and dawns may
    gleam
And purple and crimson radiance
    stream
  When day is low in the west;
And plumes of the birds of summer-
    land,
  Freighted with many a prayer,
We bring to help the spirit's way
  In the pathless depths of air.
But we do not fear that silent flight,
  Nor the slumber lone and chill;
For the Home of the Dead has song
    and love,
  And they wander where they will;
And morn and eve, by hearth and
    wood,
  We see their faces still.
Thus, day and night, and night and day,
  Our rites the Gods enchain,
And bring us peace no others win

The Ancient People

Of all their earthly train;
For we are the Ancient People,
  Born with the wind and rain.

And yet . . . and yet . . . on the
    mesa top
  As we sit when the sun is low,
And, far to west, Francisco's peaks
  Blaze in his parting glow, —
While plain, and rock, and cedar-
    steep
Fade slow from rose to gray,
And the sand-clouds, blown by the
    flying wind,
  Like demons chase the day;
And the fires of the wandering mete-
    ors gleam,
  And the dire mirage looms far
To beckon us hence to the nameless
    land
  Where our Lost Others are;

And, weird as the wail by the Spirit
    Lake
Bewildered hunters know,
The cry of the owl comes mournful up
    From the dusky glen below, —
That boding cry when death is nigh
    And days that are dim with woe; —
Sit, and think that but ruins mark
    The realm that erst was ours,
The countless cities wrapped in dust
    Which once were stately powers,
And that over our race, as over the
    plain,
    The gathering darkness lowers;
And see how great from the Sunrise-
    land
    You come with every boon,
We know that ours is the waning,
    And yours is the waxing moon!
Know that our grief and yearning
    prayers,

The Ancient People

As reeds in the blast, are vain,
And with arrows of keenest anguish
  Our tortured hearts are slain;
For we are the Ancient People,
  Born with the wind and rain!

But the same Earth spreads for us and
      you,
  And death for both is one;
Why should we not be brothers true
  Before our day is done?
You are many and great and strong;
  We, only a remnant weak;
Our heralds call at sunset still,
Yet ah, how few on plain or hill
  The evening councils seek!
And words are dead and lips are dumb
  Our hopeless woe to speak.
For the fires grow cold, and the dances
      fail,
  And the songs in their echoes die;

And what have we left but the graves
  beneath,
And, above, the waiting sky? —
Our fathers sought these frowning
  cliffs
  To rid them of their foes,
And thrice and more, on the mesa
  floor,
  Our terraced towns uprose ;
But when the stress of war was past,
  To the lowlands glad we went,
For the plain — the plain is our
  domain,
  The home of our hearts' content ;
And here, O brothers, let us dwell
  And find at last repose,
By towering Tä-ai-yal'-lo-ne,
  And the river that westward goes !
For the roads were long and rough we
  trod
  To our fields of clustering corn,

And our women grew old ere youth
    was spent,
  As wearily, night and morn,
They climbed the steep with the
    earthen jars,
  Slow-filled, to the very brim,
From the trickling springs at the
    mesa foot
  In the willow thickets dim.
Time was when seen from the loftiest
    peak
  The realm was all our own,
And only the words of the Á-shi-wi
  To the four winds were known; —
Ours were the veins of silver;
  The rivers' bounteous flow
Filling the maze of our water-ways
  From the heights to the vales below;
The plains outspreading to the sky,
  The crags, the cañon's gloom,
The cedar shades, the piñon groves,

The Ancient People

The mountain meadow's bloom ;
Nay, even the very Sun was ours,
 Above us circling slow !
And now . . . and now . . . from the
  lowest hill
 Your pastures we descry ;
Your speech is borne on every breeze
 That blows the mesas by ;
Our deep canals are furrows faint
 On the wide and desert plain ;
Of the grandeur of our temple-walls
 But mounds of earth remain,
And over our altars and our graves
 Your towns rise proud and high !
The bison is gone, and the antelope
 And the mountain sheep will follow,
And all our lands your restless bands
 Will search from height to hollow ;
And the world we knew and the life
  we lived
 Will pass as the shadows fly

The Ancient People

When the morning wind blows fresh
      and free
  And daylight floods the sky.
Alas for us who once were lords
  Of stream and peak and plain ! . . .
By ages done, by Star and Sun,
  We will not brook disdain !
No ! though your strength were thou-
      sand-fold
From farthest main to main ;
For we are the Ancient People,
  Born with the wind and rain !

Commentary
of a Zuni Familiar

By F. H. CUSHING

Commentary

IN commenting upon this Song of the
Ancient People, one is strongly tempted to
treat it in the mood and with the characteristic turns of phrase of a Zuñi Familiar.
The poem itself seems to invite such a
course, — so ancient is it in spirit and
feeling, so true to the thought and the lore
of the people it speaks for. It may be
likened to a torchlight borne through the
deep reaches of a primeval forest at mid-
night, giving vivid glimpses of the teem-
ing mythic forms of ancient Pueblo fancy
and wisdom ; so many and so representa-
tive are the points which Miss Proctor, in
briefly touching them, has illumined with
her genius. My slender excuse for the
following commentary is the desire to ex-
pand some of the brief allusions of her
poem ; to carry the light now and then
somewhat further along the forest trail,
and get a fuller view of the creatures of

27

primeval fancy. To explore the whole labyrinth of myth and imagery native to the Ancient People would require many stout volumes. In the little that is here added to Miss Proctor's verses I can but bear witness to her strict fidelity of statement, and attempt to show, as one of the Ancient People themselves would be glad to show, how well she has divined their spirit.

Let me seize this opportunity for saying a word about the poetry of primitive men. We can hardly emphasize too strongly the fact — to which many people are quite blind — that but for our slender inheritance traditionally, and our still more slender inheritance emotionally, of the mood of primeval humanity, all that is best in modern poetry would be lost. When I give but a poor translation of some ancient Zuñi epos or myth, I often hear the incredulous remark: " It cannot be that those people are so poetical. Surely it is impossible for them, without the art of writing, to give such finished and measured, even rhythmic expression to their thoughts ! "

It must be remembered that to one of

the Ancient People everything is symbolic; even the wind itself is breath and can speak; all natural phenomena are either personalities or personal acts. Such conceptions are woven into the very fibre of his speech, and dramatized in the very acts of his daily life. The symbolic interpretation of nature results in myth, the dramaturgic presentation of myth results in the dance and song of measured words; and thus among the Zuñis have arisen an astonishing number of epic recitations which, but for their too intense solemnity and their lofty disregard of the merely human element in the story, might fairly be classed with the Eddas of our Scandinavian ancestors. I am sure they would not lose by the comparison. It is quite right, therefore, that in giving us the utterances of the Ancient People the modern poet should clothe them with rhythm and rhyme, and call her poem a " Song."

If my commentary upon the poem is dictated mainly by what I know of the Zuñi people, and is rendered as the utterance of one of themselves, it need not be feared that my statements will fail to apply

to the people of the other pueblos as well.
The Zuñis are as ancient as any of these
peoples, and even to-day they enjoy a
kind of preëminence. More than half of
their mythic lore and phrases have been
adopted by the more primitive Tusayan
Indians (Moquis) of Arizona, and much
has been taken from them by the more
modernized pueblos of the Rio Grande.

With Miss Proctor I can say these ancient peoples all call the Sun their Father,
and never fail to speak of him as such.
It was said by their ancient seers : Before
aught was, before even Time began to be,
the Holder of the Trails of Life, whose
person is the Sun, whose bright shield we
see each shining day, — before aught was,
save void space and darkness, He was.
And by thinking he wrought light, and
with light he dispelled the darkness, whence
descended clouds and water, even as from
the night fall mists of the morning laden
with moisture. Into these life-sustaining
waters he dropped the seed of his being,
whence sprang the Sky-Father and the
Earth-Mother. Born of these twain were
all creatures here below, numberless on

the plains, as in the sky. Born of his sister, the Moon-Mother, were the lesser stars, themselves our brothers paternal even as we are their brothers younger.

The Red Men, dusky with the darkness of their birth from the fourfold womb of the Earth-Mother, and ruddy with the life she gave them, were the earliest born of men. Even the seven wind-making Grandsires came forth with them, and they brought the seeds of rain and storm. Such were our fathers, — fathers of the *man-races* of men. For when your fathers came from over the Sea of Sunrise, they were white like the Dawn whom they followed, and weakly withal like women, and in these our deserts they often died of thirst. Wherefore said our ancient seers: These palefaces must be our younger brothers, the *woman-men* born on the other side of the world, when, after giving birth to us, our Earth-Mother turned over, perchance that she might give birth to them. Yet how could ye have been born had not the Twain own children of the Sun, the Warriors of Chance, descended and planted the world-canes in the nethermost womb of

Earth, that, by climbing as on ladders, our unfinished fathers and the creatures with them might be brought forth?

Even as they led them forth, the Twain Beloved taught certain Chosen Ones concerning the substance and meaning of things high and low. And they said unto the Chosen Ones: Fear not the serpent shafts of the lightning as they rattle loudly, that the earth be replenished with their children the serpents of water, the rivers of life. Fear not the light of the Sun-Father, though at first it seemeth to blind and to blight, for beneath him he carries his shield, so that the world is not seared as he journeys along the path of day, — the path that leads to the hollow mountain of the sunset sea where he dies. But that is his mother-home, and when he enters it he is straightway born anew in the Underworld; yet again, when night is done, to be born through the hollow mountain of the sunrise sea, his father-home.

It is then at sunrise — after the nine days of their nativity are numbered — that the sisters of mothers carry forth the new-born babes with fervent prayers and breathings to receive the young light and new breath of the ever-ancient but again new-born Sun-Father ; and as he is newly come from his father-home, so these little ones are now first given into the arms of their father's sisters, and named with the names of their childhood. Thus even as the Father of the Day is a new-made child in the morning, even so we pray that the light of his birth may linger long upon them ere they have their setting.

We have learned why the Moon, fair bride of the Sun, is thus the mother of all maternity, and why, therefore, so often at night she leans forth over the terraced shores of the sky ocean, and reaches her white arms down toward now some, now others, of the mothers of men, according to their appointed days of sacrifice in Her waxing and waning; while her younger sister, Goddess of the White Shells, beckons to men, — telling them that all maidens may become daughters of her elder sister, as their own mothers became, won by love-presents of her white shells from the shores of her home in the sea.

Commentary

Our ancients tell how the Twain Beloved who first guided them forth from the Under-world became warriors, — grim and misshapen, so ugly that all maidens jeered at them. Yet, forsooth, they would rival all youths!

"What are the most beautiful flowers that grow?" said one. "The seven-hued flowers of Té-na-tsa-li," said the other. "Lo! we will seek him afar!" They found a measuring-worm greater than any ever seen by man. They called him "Grandfather," and with other winsome words won him to help them.

"Sit ye astride me, little fellows," said he. Then he arched his back with such mighty strain that he stretched himself to the sky, and, plunging westward, reached even to the far mountain of Té-na-tsa-li! There they found Té-na-tsa-li, aged and white-haired with all the winters that had ever been. And long they shouted ere He heard them, so old was he! Hearing, he passed his hand before his breast, breathing mists, whence he issued, a youth glorious and happy to see, young with all the springtimes that had ever been. Flowers

34

were growing bright and fresh from his head-dress. Flowers sprang up all around his mountain from the mists of his breath. " Pluck these!" he said, smiling gladly. And they plucked countless flowers from his head-dress, and countless the flowers grew where they had plucked. But when they returned to A′-mi-to-lan-ne, the measuring-worm, he was devouring the flowers at the foot of the mountain. " Nay, I will not bear ye back," said he, "ere I have plucked all these flowers ; for so great am I grown with my journey that no forest would surfeit my hunger."

" But we will deck thee, Grandfather, with some of these brighter ones ; and for food, consume the clouds of the sky as erstwhile thou didst the forest leaves."

Then he bore them back swiftly. And with their flowers they won the smiles of all maidens whose favor they chose to win. But, decked by the flowers they left on him, the measuring-worm of the skies sprang aloft, streaking the full length of his body with all their glorious colors. Fadeless these hues as the sun, for, as then he consumed the bright rain-clouds and drew up the life of all flowers, so ever it is to this day.

Evil and good are the gods, even as men. The Morning Star, elder of the Beloved Twain who descended, gives strength to the Bearers of Bows, and wakes them at the most fearsome time of the morning. The Sun - Father, following, makes the world new each day, giving new life to all men, and the light of wisdom to his favored children ; while the Moon-Mother renews life from month to month and generation to generation. But the lightning — good from Wi'-lo-lo-a-ne — is deadly when sent by A'-nah-si-a-na, wielder of thunder - bolts ; so we cut their jagged swift lines on our arrows that these may be made certain and fatal by the power of likeness. And we paint on our shields the hated bright form of A'-mi-to-lan-ne, consumer of clouds, that our enemies, seeing it and dreading, may be withered as by him are green-growing things. Terrible is the Whirlwind Man-Eagle of the skies, winding down from on high and striding over the earth. His form, and the form of his younger brother, the Eagle, whose plumes

36

we wear, we also paint on our war-gear.
For our Fathers of the Bow were taught
the potency of dread symbols.

So, the fathers of our other sacred assemblies were taught that with feather-
stroking and fearless thought they could
quell the anger of a venomed serpent, or
command the fiercest beasts at night-time,
with magic circles of yucca and crystals of
divination. For by mystic motions and
the power of the eye, they could draw their
souls forth in the moonlight, and through
those loops of rebirth enter their bodies
and learn all their ways; yea, and the craft
of their gods themselves. So learned they
of the great mountain lion of the North-
land how to subdue alike the elk or the
strong bison, how even to stay the flight of
the grouse over the snow; so of the bear
and coyote, masters of the Westland, how
to overreach even the mountain sheep;
and so of the wild-cat and the badger, masters of the Southland, how to capture the
red deer and draw fire from the cedar;
and of the gray, gaunt wolf-god of the
Eastland they learned how his children
overtake the fleet-footed comrades of the

dawn on far mesas, the antelopes ; so, too, of the eagle-god of the Over-world, how to be, as are his children, far-sighted and unfailing ; and of the preymole and gopher, masters of the Under-world, how their children burrow pitfalls for unwary walkers. Gods, all of these, of all the Six Regions, in semblance of beasts who command separately in each.

Magical as were our fathers, neither the master - gods, nor their messengers the beast-gods, would show aught to others than their own children among men, the elders of the clans named after themselves, and they willed not that their secrets be revealed to any others. Wherefore we have sacred assemblies of wise priests — of the North, twain brotherhoods, wielders of cold, makers of war ; of the West, world of waters, twain also, — holders of the seed of rain and spring making ; of the South, twain, — masters of fire and scourgers of sorcery and fevered sickness ; of the East, twain holders of the seed of soil, of the secret of maturing, interpreters of the meaning of light to the Spirits of Men ; of the Over-world twain, — priests of the eagle-kind, and of daylight to mortals; and of the Under-world twain, — priests of the serpent and darkness, who know how begotten are all seeds and beings. These be the four brotherhoods of Winter, Spring, Summer, and Autumn; of the medicines of Air, Water, Fire and Earth, whereby all beings live; and the two brotherhoods of the two states wherein all things and all creatures are, — waking or sleeping, — Light and Darkness. But over them all and wiser than all are our seven foremost fathers, guardians and priests of the prayers, songs and dances of our sacred A'-kâ-kâ; first, the six masters of the regions six, then the Father of them all, Priest Speaker of the Sun, and the Mother of us all, Priestess Keeper of their seed, for they are of the mid-most place.

So wise are these our fathers, that they can tell us why, when serpents, younger brothers of the Lightning, have stilled their rattling, the Thunder too is hushed, and the Bear lazily sleeps, no longer guarding the Westland from the cold of the Ice-gods and the white down of their mighty breathing. How, when the Bear awaking,

growls in springtime and the answering
thunders mutter, the strength of the Ice-
gods being shaken, the flute of Pai'-ya-
tu-ma, god of dew and the dawn, sounds
afar, and the breath of his corn-maidens
singing, comes warm from the Southland.
Lo ! their song-birds and butterflies, dancing to their music, forthwith bring Summer. Then they tell us 't is the time to
pluck the flowers of Té-na-tsa-li, renewer
of seasons, whose flesh in the flowers renews our flesh, as his breath in their fra-
grance makes this the time of growing.

Our fathers, priests of the Over-world
and seers, teach us of things afar, and the
hidden meanings they divine with the crystals we find, and they tell us of the sky-
hero, God of the Turquoise ; how, when
mortals became greedy of his gifts and
importunate, he wearied, as did his bride,
the white-plumed Goddess of Salt. So, together they fled away, and wherever rained
the sweat of their journey, on hilltop or
mountain, it hardened to salt and turquoises.

Our fathers of the midmost place, master priests of the six sacred Kiva-Houses,

go forth when the Sun-Priest calls them from the housetops, and with prayer-meal mark out the lines of the Six Regions whereby we shall plant our first corn hills ; and they counsel for us our plumed prayer-wands, that the Beings of all the great spaces may see in these plumes winged with meaning the needs of our children and corn-plants.

Alas ! when we plant not these plumes with our hearts as well as before the eyes of men, no more may be seen the night-god of new waters, the Toad with the markings of turquoise, of coral and sun-shine on water. Nay, he sleeps in the Earth, until with labor and fasting our hearts are made right, and until by wor-ship in song and dance and with the sound of flutes and drums, we invoke the beloved Rain Gods until they must needs grant our beseechings. Then the Toad, appear-ing, wins further their favor.

"Be ye true," said the Gods when time was new, "Be ye true, and by these things we give you, and by the customs we teach you, ye shall have power, even over our-selves." And lo ! our fathers in that time toiled sleeplessly, nor feared they pain, that they might still their hearts of all other longing save to gain these things.

All that they sought and gained has been yearly untied from the strands of song and story kept unbroken through all the lives of men by our sacred assemblies, and by the fathers of the Kâ'-kâ. For, as did our ancients, so do these, labor and watch and fast enduringly through all appointed nights, keeping silence by day, that their sacred thoughts may be unbroken and their hearts be kept likewise true. So, in the perfection of their lives, our precious forms and things of the gods are kept potent, and even we are fitted to bring them at times into the sacred precincts of the shrines of all the Six Regions, and to join there our fathers in their vigils and fasts, and with our dances and songs to aid the power of their incantations and prayers.

But even in the sight of these our fathers, we are poor of heart and halting of speech concerning sacred things. Wherefore, our fathers purify us with water and honey - dust consecrated by their living

Commentary

breaths, and bid us wear all of our trea-
sures from sea, earth, and sky, shells of the
ocean, turquoises of the mountains, and
plumes of the eagle and birds of the summer ; to apparel ourselves only in the dress
of our Fair Goddess of Cotton, robes broid-
ered brightly with symbols of meaning
which shall speak for us — speak with the
figured vases, wands and mantles we bear
into the presence ; speak for us and save
us from fear and disfavor, when at the call
of their dread but beloved names, the
Mighty Gods from the far Regions lay
hold of their parts in our altars. By these
fulfilments of our worship we win all gifts,
not corn alone, but length of life. Aye,
we live, live, though for ages danger and
war have sore encompassed us here in the
midmost place.

Even so said the Twain Beloved when
they led men forth into daylight, and the
borders of the world were new and all un-
stable with earthquakes and thunder: "Seek
ye the place of the middle, the lap of the
Earth-Mother, — there only may ye bide
in safety." And they led them for countless years through far journeys. Great

43

were our people, greater and greater grew they, walking with Gods as they eastward came.

In the tales of those times their wisdom is told us. We·are their children! Until our hearths are blackened, these tales shall be told. Naught else will keep our fires from dying!

There was a man, — born ere the Twain Beloved descended. Alone he walked the Path of Day. His prayer that men be born to the sunlight was granted! But no man knew, and ages passed away. Lo! he was born again, poor and lonely, when men had grown evil. It was his prayer that he be born again, which was granted! Oh, our Master Pó-shai-an-k'ya, we did not know him! Only few knew him. These followed him to his wondrous City-in-the-Mists-Enfolded, and were taught by him all that men lacked of good; all that men knew not of the mysteries of worship; all that men needed for the ways of life. "He who lives the perfect life," said Pó-shai-an-k'ya, the master, "so living shall perfect the lives of the imperfect. He who lives the perfect life, his heart must be undi-

vided and unwavering. He who would be
heard by the silent Surpassing Ones, must
pray in his heart; speaking or not speaking, he shall be heard!" Saying such
things, — as the sinking Sun is instantly
gone, the Master left them and never came
again. But when we pray in the words he
taught us, it is His prayer that is granted!
Yea, and shall be so long as we keep burning in our hearts his sacred fire, and with
willing hands from season to season light
it anew on our altars.

The soul of the dead when but newly
done with the daylight of life is like an
awakened dreamer, dazed and seeing
naught, dumb and hearing naught. It is
lost until severed wholly from the sunlight-
life. So, we of the nearest kin break beside the still waiting soul a vase of the
water of bodily life, giving back to the Sun
at his setting the Life of Days as he gave
it in the morning of childhood, — that the
soul, set free, shall sink like him, to live
again with the souls there below the dark
waters of Kâ'-thlu-ël-lon, and, like him, rise
again to breath in the clouds here above
us. Therefore, too, we give the body to

the Earth-Mother, that it call not the soul forth to be a lonely ghost, or vex it while it is taking part in the glad councils and dances of the Ancients. So also we plant by the river-side plumes of the westward-winging summer-birds, as the signs of Life and of the way and of our prayers, to waft the unwakened soul thither, and speak for it whilst as yet it knows not the life of the Lake of Spirits. Verily we lie down to the sleep of fulfilment fearlessly and well content. We do not forget that the lightning is not dimmed by the darkness. It but gleams the more brightly. Even so is it with the souls of men in the night-time of death.

* * * * *

The ruined towns of the Ancient People lie scattered throughout the valleys and plains of our vast southwest. Whilst some of these mark the paths of their slow migrations, others were their homes for ages. This was conclusively shown by the extensive and careful excavations continued for nearly two years by the Hemenway Archæological Expedition, in some of the ancient cities or great clusters of pueblos in southern Arizona. There, in the lower plain of the Salado River alone, I found and examined some thirteen of these Pueblo cities. Each of them was buried from sight save for a great solitary earth mound which stood surrounded by low, wide-reaching and seemingly natural undulations of the soil. Traversing the plain almost from border to border were wavering, faint lines of water-stones, and here and there dim furrows. These — so it proved later — showed the courses of canals, once well lined with hardened clay. Each slightest elevation around the great mounds covered the foundations of many-roomed houses, while the central mounds themselves proved to be great Kiva-Temples. The arrangement of the rooms in these was so like the plans marked out in prayer-meal for priestly ceremonials in Zuñi to-day, and the paraphernalia we unearthed from them were so like what is used in these same Zuñi ceremonials, that one must needs believe the builders of those and uncounted other such cities to have been near kindred to the Zuñis, at least in culture. Believing, as the Zuñis do, that they were more than this, that these ruins were the homes of their own ancestors and " Lost Others," — those who faltered in seeking the Middle of the World, and so drifted away southward, no one knows whither, — we cannot wonder that they speak of theirs as the " Waning Moon," likening us palefaces in number to those same dead ancestors and Lost Others.

And again, if one thinks as they so often think, of the times when they fled from their beloved plain at the middle of the world, and rebuilt on the broad and lofty summit of Thunder Mountain their citadels of stone, and that in those days as far as the eye could reach from their topmost terrace, all the plains and valleys were their own possessions, stoutly held in stress of war at fearful odds ; we can imagine what they think and feel to-day when all too easily they look across the narrow strip of land we let them call their own. Miss Proctor tells us in words so like their own that it seems almost vain to add another. Yet this is what their old men say : —

" Beasts in a tempest do not bellow at

the wind; they know it would not heed them! Let us then turn our backs to the coming time of stormy thoughts, our faces to the mighty past of our ancients, — that past which never ceases, — that we may remember we are their children, and be strong yet a little longer."

In such wise do the old men answer when some one younger wonders how it will seem when they are all like "Americans," as some Americans promise they shall be. "Ye will not be like them," I once heard a venerable sage reply, "ye will be dead! Aye, and 't is better so!"

𝕹𝖔𝖙𝖊𝖘

By JOHN FISKE

Notes

1. "*Ours is the ancient wisdom.*" — The *kiva*, better known to us, perhaps, by its Spanish name *estufa*, is, among other things, the university, or perhaps we might say the divinity school, of the Pueblo. Here the young man is orally instructed in all the sacred rites and ceremonies of his people, their genesis and their traditions. So careful are they that no mistakes shall be made, the youth is obliged to go over, day after day and year after year, these oral instructions and the long rituals, until he is able to repeat them without the loss of a sentence or word, thereby proving himself qualified to succeed the older men of his people, and so transmit this sacred knowledge to coming generations.

The picture represents a daily occurrence in the kiva life. The priests have taken their proper places about the flat altar, where a small fire is kept burning; a youth stands before them, in class, so to speak, receiving his lesson.

Notes

Among the Moquis, the kiva is excavated out of the rock below the surface of the mesa, and then covered over, leaving an opening through which descent is made by a ladder. The kivas of the Zuñi and the Pueblos of the Rio Grande are built above the ground, although entrance to them is made from the top, as with the Moquis.

In each Pueblo there are as many kivas as there are groups or classes of esoteric societies ; as, for example, the orders of the Antelope, the Snake, the Bear, the Eagle, etc., etc. The basket, *co-ja-ni-na* (people of the Willows), so called from the tribe that live at the foot of Cataract Cañon, among the heavy grove of willows that grow there, contains *pe-ki*, the native bread, of a slate color. The embroidered sash is used in ceremonies. The jar, or *olla*, containing water, can be found in all the kivas when work is going on.

The men all smoke during their ceremonies, sometimes their ancient pipes, but more generally cigarettes.

2. *The Sun-god*, the chief deity of the Pueblo Indians, is believed to be the Father of all men. He dies every evening with the setting, and is born anew every morning with the rising sun. " The Sun-father, soaring above the

sun, moon, and stars, . . . is surrounded by the symbols of the principal phenomena in nature that are regarded as essentially beneficent to mankind." (Bandelier, *The Delight Makers*, p. 147.)

2. "*We carry our new-born children forth.*" — Among the Moqui Indians, it is customary, twenty days after the birth of a child, to introduce the infant to the sun. The godmother, after wrapping the baby in an old blanket, and placing it in its cradle, laces the child, together with an ear of corn, snugly in its place.

The father watches for the coming of the sun, and when he announces its faintest appearance, the godmother with the child, followed by the mother, steps out of the house, and they stand on each side of the door, the mother at the right, the godmother at the left. They both scatter sacred meal as the sun appears. As soon as the child has been thus presented they retire into the house, where their relatives are awaiting them. For a complete account of this ceremony, see the article "Natal Ceremonies of the Hopi Indians," by J. G. Owens, in the *Journal of American Ethnology and Archæology*, vol. ii. p. 163. In Zuñi the ceremony, which is very similar, is performed on the tenth day. See Mrs. Stevenson, "Religious Life of a Zuñi Child," in *Fifth Report of the Bureau of Ethnology*.

3. "*A'-mi-to-lan-ne*" is one of the Zuñi names for rainbow. There are distinct Rainbow gods and goddesses, as there are distinct Lightning deities. Nearly all phenomena, personified as gods, are in a measure regarded as animals, and of each kind there are apt to be many, male and female, good and evil. Thus the principal Rainbow god is a male, "false and cruel" like the "ruthless worm" that devours the buds. He is called "consumer of clouds," "stealer of the thunder-ball," etc. On the other hand the "Rainbow of the Mist," *A'-mi-to-la-ni-tsa*, is a fertile female, a kinswoman of the Dew or Morning-Mist. She is the bearer of salubrious breaths and good tidings from "Those Above," i. e., the immortal Cosmic Gods.

4. "*The Corn-maids*" are mythological beings supposed to give fertility to the soil and foster the growth of the corn. In the Corn-Drama they are personated by virgins regarded as their own human sisters.

During the planting season, and until the ripening of the corn, these virgins are frequently employed in watching the fields, that the ravens may not raid them and destroy the prospect of a crop. They build bowers of cotton-wood limbs, for shade, and in these make their summer homes, having with them their blankets and furs, and such needlework as they occupy their time with. The picture is from a sketch made in the Zuñi basin, some six miles from the Pueblo.

The costumes of all the Pueblo women are quite the same. All the blanket-dresses are made by the Moquis, and sold by them among the other Pueblos. Sometimes they receive money in return, but more often ponies, shell beads, turquoise beads, silver ornaments made by the Navajos, and larger and more fanciful blankets for general covering.

In this picture of the Zuñi girls one can fancy one's self looking at a bevy of Moqui maidens (barring the cart-wheel puffs), or any of the young women of the Pueblos of the Rio Grande. The type is the same among them all.

5. "*The eagle, bird of the Whirlwind-God*," figures often in Zuñi folk-tales, where he performs marvelous feats. "Eagle feathers are highly esteemed for religious purposes. Eagles are kept in wattled corrals on the west side of Zuñi Pueblo, in the plaza near the church, and here and there throughout the Pueblo, some-

times even on the housetops, without cages. They are often sorry-looking birds, poorly representing an emblem of national power." (J. W. Fewkes, *Journal of American Ethnology and Archæology*, vol. ii. p. 26.)

5. "*Wile the wolf from his den.*" — The Indians have peculiar calls which they use in alluring game within shooting distance of the bow and arrow ; and sometimes so close that they can dispatch a wolf or coyote with their stone axes.

The call which allures the wolf is the peculiar sound uttered by the female wild turkey. Then they use the bone of the turkey leg for a whistle, with which they imitate various birds, calling the larger ones by uttering the notes of the small ones, upon which they prey. These are the methods most obvious to us, but regarded by the Indian as comparatively clumsy. Priests of the hunter societies, through their intimate knowledge of animal habits and aptitudes, exhibit remarkable powers of charming beasts and birds. They sometimes produce effects analogous to hypnotism. Mr. Cushing tells me that he has seen prairie-dogs lured out to the edges of their burrows by cries half-imitative, half-musical ; and then held motionless there by the flashing of light into their eyes from prisms of rock-crystal, until they became stupefied and could be captured alive.

The landscape in this picture is from the butte and cañon country of northern Arizona.

7. " *The lilies of Té-na-tsa-li.*" — This person is the hero of a folk-tale. He attempted to woo a lovely maiden, who, with her three beautiful sisters, lived at Kiakima on Thunder Mountain. These maidens were very rich, and made beautiful baskets. Many young men tried to woo them, but each one disappeared mysteriously, having been killed by these cruel but beautiful girls. Té-na-tsa-li, a child of the gods, the brother of the god of Dew, loved the elder one, and went to her house. The maiden said if he could hide from her so she could not find him, then she would wed him; but he, knowing her magic arts, refused to go first, and insisted upon her hiding from him. This she tried to do, but by means of magic he found her. Then he tried to hide from her, but, knowing that she could find him, by magic, anywhere on earth, he mounted on a sun's ray to the Sun-father. The maiden followed his footsteps till they stopped, and then, filling a shell with water, looked into it and saw the reflection of the sun, and Té-na-tsa-li hidden there. When he found he was discovered, Té-na-tsa-li

came to the earth again, and asked the maiden what her commands were. Without answering she drew a sharp obsidian knife from her robe and cut off his head, buried the body, and dragged the bleeding head to her house, where she hid it. As Té-na-tsa-li did not return home, his brother went to find him, and was able to trace him by the beautiful flowers which had sprung up where he had stepped or his blood had dropped. The bright-colored lilies which grow near Zuñi are called the lilies of Té-na-tsa-li, and are said to have the power to heal the sick and those who have suffered in war. (Abridged from a Zuñi folk-tale, translated by F. H. Cushing.)

7. "*Plant the earliest maize.*" — In aboriginal American mythology the beautiful Indian corn plays as prominent a part as the cow in ancient Aryan folk-lore. Dr. Fewkes observes that "this characteristic American plant may rightly be called the natural food of all the Pueblo people. Their folk-tales teem with references to it, and it is regarded as one of the best gifts of the gods. Their language is rich in names for maize in its different stages of growth, and for the products made from it."

7. "*Prayer-plumes*" are "painted sticks to which the feathers or down of various birds

(according to the nature of the prayer they are to signify) are attached. The aborigine deposits these wherever and whenever he feels like addressing himself to the higher powers, be it for a request, in adoration only, or for thanksgiving. In a certain way the prayer-plume or plume-stick is a substitute for prayer, inasmuch as he who has not time may deposit it hurriedly as a votive offering. The paint which covers the piece of stick to which the feather is attached becomes appropriately significant through its colors ; the feather itself is the symbol of human thought, flitting as one set adrift in the air toward heaven, where dwell those above." (Bandelier, *The Delight Makers*, p. 100.)

"While she stands and gazes and dreams, a flake of down becomes detached, and quivers upward in the direction of the moon's silvery orb. Such a flitting and floating plume is the symbol of prayer. It rises and rises, and at last disappears as if absorbed by moonlight. The mother above has listened to her entreaty, for the symbol of her thought, the feather, has gone to rest in the bosom of her who watches over every house, who feels with every loving, praying heart." (*Ibid.* p. 154.)

7. "*As full to the east we kneel.*" — The ceremony of planting *ba-hos* (prayer-sticks) at the

watering-places is common among all the Pueblo Indians. A certain order, called Kō-Kō, is composed partly of unmarried women, who take a vow of celibacy before entering the order. They repair to the springs before dawn, and place the ba-hos about the water. This is to invoke the aid of the water-god to send them plenty of rain, that their crops may be bountiful.

The feathers attached to the ba-hos symbolize thought, and in this ceremony waft their prayers to the water-god above ; the sticks to which the feathers are attached are fashioned to represent lightning, the water-deity.

The Pueblo Indians, not being able to separate the subjective from the objective, recognize a likeness between the snake and the lightning, therefore they are related ; and for this reason we account for their high veneration of the snake. They believe lightning to be the water-god himself. When he appears he strikes a cloud, and the report of the blow is the thunder which follows ; the effect is rain.

This ceremony is performed two or three or more times a year, according to the condition of the weather. Drought will bring the Kō-Kō together for this ceremony more frequently, of course.

Prayer-sticks of similar construction to the ba-ho are placed about the graves of the departed.

7. *"And the water-god, the jeweled toad."* — In the Southwest during and after a rain the beautiful desert toads come to the surface, and when wet their bodies reflect the light and shine like jewels. The Indians believed that these toads had power to bring rain, and so they used to make images of toads which they placed along their watercourses to guide the water. Very few of these fetishes are known to exist now; but beautiful ancient specimens, encrusted with turquoises and coral-shells inlaid in gum, were found by the Hemenway Expedition in the buried Pueblos of the Salado valley.

9. *"The dance and prayers of the A'-kâ-kâ."* — The A'-kâ-kâ (called *Ka-tcí-nas* by the Moquis) is the brotherhood of the Mythic-Drama-Dance, and its members represent symbolically the souls of the first ancestors of mankind. For further accounts see Mrs. Stevenson, "Religious Life of a Zuñi Child," in *Fifth Report of the Bureau of Ethnology.*

11. *" Crosses, terraces, slanting bars."* — "The red cross is the symbol of the morning star; the white, of the evening. The terraced pyramids are the clouds, for the clouds appear to

the Indian as staircases leading to heaven, and they in turn support the rainbow, a tri-colored arch." (Bandelier, *The Delight Makers*, p. 147.)

12. " *Twin children of the Sun.*" — There is a tradition among the Zuñi and Moqui Indians that two youths, called " twin children of the Sun," bade adieu to their people, and started upon a pilgrimage to find where day began. They were never heard of afterward, but it is supposed they are now the guests of the Ka-tcí-nas. They are the " Twain-Beloved " mentioned in the Zuñi Familiar's *Commentary*.

These young men are represented in the traditional primitive costume of the cougar skin, bow and quiver, and the eagle feather.

12. "*Pó-shai-an-k'ya, the master.*" — A great character in Zuñi mythology, the leader and saviour of the people. See Mr. Cushing's *Commentary*, above, p. 42. The conception of Pó-shai-an-k'ya, as here presented by Mr. Cushing, suggests the query whether it does not betray the influence of Christian ideas.

15. " *The silent heart's appeal.*" — Mr. Scott's picture is an Arizona scene, the site of one of the ancient cities, the ruins of which the Indians maintain have always been ruins ; no traditions exist among them of a time when they were standing, and were the abode of men.

The figure is a middle-aged woman who has had trouble; she has ascended the high mesa to where the altar stands, and is alone with her sorrow. These altars are found in an almost perfect state of preservation (so sacred are they held by all the Indians) among the vast ruined towns that are found on the mesa tops that skirt the valleys of Arizona and New Mexico.

15. *"The rare tobacco leaves."* — Dr. Fewkes says (*Journal*, vol. iii. p. 76) that native tobacco was used in the sacred ceremonials. Although he supplied the Indians plentifully with white men's tobacco, he never saw them use it in sacred rites. The bark of the red willow is often used in place of tobacco.

16. *" By the dead a vase of water clear."*— It is the custom to break a bowl of clear water beside the dead, that the soul may have an easy and speedy passage to the other world.

16. *"Through Kâ-thlu-el'-lon's Lake."* — This is a sacred lake about sixty miles southwest of Zuñi, through which the A'-kâ-kâ are believed to have come up on the earth, and through which, after death, the soul passes to Shi-papu, where there is eternal dancing and feasting.

18. *"Far to west, Francisco's peaks."*— Mr. Scott's picture is a view under the mesa of Shi-

mo-pa-vi. The man is going for wood ten miles away across the desert, while the girls, on their way to the spring, are waving him a good-by.

The pueblo of Shi-mo-pa-vi is the loftiest of the Moqui villages. From its walls there is a glorious view of the desert, with the snow-capped peaks of the Francisco Mountains in central Arizona, the range whence the Francisco River winds its way down to the Gila and the weird Colorado, until its waters are lost in the Vermilion Sea, as the old explorers used to call the Gulf of California. These mountains have nothing to do with *San Francisco*, from which they are distant many hundred miles; nor do they belong even to the Sierra Nevada, but to the Rocky Mountain system.

The picture is taken from the upper terrace of the mesa. There are three terraces below as one descends to the sand dunes and *débris* at the base, where you may still see the ruins of the old town of Shi-mo-pa-vi, destroyed in warfare three centuries ago. Its ancient watering-places still remain, and supply the present pueblo.

20. "*We are the Ancient People.*" — The picture is a view of the Pueblo of Wálpi, which is the most southerly village on the first Moqui

mesa; it is upon the terminal point of the mesa, eight hundred feet above the desert. Here the famous biennial snake dance takes place about the Sacred Rock in front of the Pueblo.

The rock about which the performance takes place can be seen directly in front of the lowest white dwelling.

The stone corrals in the foreground are for the sheep which are taken down to the desert and back daily.

The mesa just above the corrals is only about twelve feet wide, and the trail to Wálpi over this part has been worn to eight and ten inches deep by bare feet and soft moccasins.

20. *"Our heralds call at sunset still."* — It is still the custom in Zuñi and Moqui for the herald, who is a kind of town crier, to announce events, make known the loss of goods, etc.

21. *"By towering Tä-ai-yal'-lo-ne."* — Midway between the gateway of Zuñi and the Cañon of Cottonwoods stands majestic Thunder Mountain, Tä-ai-yal'-lo-ne, magnificent in the coloring and chiseling of its rocky sides. From its hill-ensconced base to its almost level summit, the height is about a thousand feet. At the foot stand the ruins of the ancient

Zuñi town of Kiakima. It was near this spot that the negro Estevánico, companion of Fray Marcos of Nizza, was killed by the Zuñis in 1539. See Fiske, *Discovery of America*, vol. ii. p. 505.

22. "*The trickling springs at the mesa foot.*" — All the water at Moqui has to be carried up to a height of seven hundred feet from the springs at the foot of the mesa. Morning and evening the women meet at the watering-places to fill their large canteens and ollas, or earthen jars. They take the occasion for rest and gossip, and, after all, while their lives are full of toil, they seem careless and happy, and certainly enjoy themselves more than when put among civilized people whose advanced condition they cannot at all comprehend.

It is extremely interesting to go to the springs early in the morning or at close of day and study the groups that collect by them. At first they are shy and restrained by the presence of a stranger, but on acquaintance they resume their natural ways, and begin to chatter and frolic.

The Moqui women dress their hair in different ways to distinguish a maiden from a married woman. The former wears upon the side of her head, just above the ears, huge cart-wheel puffs, while the married women and old women wear theirs braided, banged, tied in a knot behind, or allowed to drop loosely by the sides. The Spaniards noticed these cart-wheel puffs in 1539. No other Pueblo women have adopted this peculiar way of distinguishing the maidens.

This scene is from under the second Moqui mesa.

22. "*A'-shi-wi*" is a Zuñi name for the Zuñis themselves.

23. " *The mountain meadow's bloom.*" -- In the Zuñi Mountains there are little meadows where the deer used to graze, and the picture represents one of these green places about twenty miles from Zuñi.

It was the ancient hunting-ground of the Zuñi Indians, and is at the present time occupied by a cattle company, whose herds have supplanted the deer and antelope of other days. In some of the valleys the pine-tree grows to very great proportions. It should be borne in mind that the altitude of these grazing spots is not less than six and seven thousand feet above the level of the sea.

www.ingramcontent.com/pod-product-compliance
Lightning Source LLC
Chambersburg PA
CBHW020409030726
47496CB00007B/2378